P9-AQU-660

The Story Of Imelda, Who Was Small

Morris Lurie

For Esther,
A book to grow into

Illustrated by
Terry Denton

Houghton Mifflin Company
Boston 1988

This is the story of Imelda, who was small. And I don't mean just a little bit small. I mean tiny. I mean absolutely tiny. I mean so absolutely tiny that she slept in a shoebox. And a very tiny shoebox it was, too.

'Good morning, Imelda!' her mother greeted her one morning, opening wide the curtains to let in the sun. 'And how are we this wonderful morning?'

Imelda brushed away a small tear from a small eye with a small hand.

'Still small,' said Imelda, in a very small voice.

'Oh dear,' said Imelda's mother sadly.

'But this is outrageous!' cried Imelda's father. 'This smallness has gone on quite long enough! It's just too embarrassing having such a small daughter! I don't like it one single bit!'

'Oh dear,' said Imelda's mother. 'But what shall we do?'

'It's off to Dr Anderson!' cried Imelda's father. 'Should have thought of it ages ago! He's a terribly tall chap, he'll know what to do! We'll go at once!'

But just then his stomach gave a rather loud rumble.

'Whoops,' said Imelda's father. 'At once after we've had our breakfast, I mean.'

And that's exactly what they did.

'Next!' cried Dr Anderson, sitting at his desk. 'Next!'

Dr Anderson's door opened a tiny crack but no one seemed to come in.

'I said next!' cried Dr Anderson. 'Come on, I haven't got all day!'

And then he saw Imelda. She was standing very quietly and very politely, feet together, head up, on the carpet in front of his desk.

'Good heavens!' cried Dr Anderson, his eyes opening so wide they looked just like two hard-boiled eggs on a plate at a picnic. 'I've never seen such a small girl in all my days! Little girl, you should see a doctor! Oops!' he said, suddenly remembering who he was and giving a little giggle. 'I am a doctor!'

Now Imelda's mother and father came in, too.

'This is our daughter, Imelda,' began Imelda's mother. 'She —'

But before Imelda's mother could say another word, Dr Anderson quickly held up a finger.

'Ssh!' he whispered.

And then he bent right down to Imelda, so close that their noses were almost touching.

'Little girl,' he said. 'Let me ask you some questions. Do you brush your hair and teeth every single day?'

'Of course!' said Imelda.

'And you never eat with your elbows on the table?'

'Never!' said Imelda.

'And you always wear socks that are both the same colour?'

'Always!' said Imelda.

'Hmmm,' said Dr Anderson, leaning back in his chair and stroking his chin. 'Seems like a perfect child to me.'

'Dr Anderson!' cried Imelda's father, who was growing impatient with all this. 'We are not here to talk about hair or teeth or elbows or socks! We've come to you about our daughter's size!'

'Oh,' said Dr Anderson. 'I was hoping you wouldn't say that. Treating small girls for being small can be quite tricky, quite tricky indeed. Oh, well. Best get on with it.' He opened a drawer in his desk, and took out an old wooden ruler and a big black book.

'This isn't going to hurt, is it?' said Imelda, looking suddenly quite frightened in her own small way.

'Hurt?' Dr Anderson laughed. 'No, no, little girl. Of course not. This is only to measure you with. Now, if you'll just stand perfectly still.'

And huffing and puffing and becoming quite red in the face, Dr Anderson got down on his hands and knees and carefully measured Imelda with his old wooden ruler from the tips of her toes to the top of her head.

'Hmmm,' he said, looking at the ruler. 'You are small, aren't you?' And he wrote down Imelda's height, which was a very small number, in his big black book.

'Now,' said Dr Anderson, 'let me tell you the secret of being tall. If you want to be tall, you must eat only long foods!'

'Long foods?' said Imelda's mother and father both together.

'Spaghetti!' said Dr Anderson.

'Goodness me!' said Imelda's mother.

'Runner beans!' said Dr Anderson.

'I say!' said Imelda's father.

'Licorice sticks!' cried Imelda.

'Yes, they're very good, too,' said Dr Anderson. 'Anything that's long is good if you want to be tall.'

'How interesting!' said Imelda's mother and father.

'Also,' said Dr Anderson, holding up a finger, 'avoid all short, dumpy foods!'

'Short, dumpy foods?' said Imelda's mother and father.

'Porridge!' said Dr Anderson.

'Naturally!' said Imelda's mother.

'Potatoes!' said Dr Anderson.

'Of course!' said Imelda's father.

'Pancakes!' cried Imelda.

'Yes, stay away from pancakes,' said Dr Anderson. 'You'll never grow tall if you eat pancakes. Well, that's the secret. Long foods and short foods! Eat one, avoid the other! Never fails! Come back in a week! Good morning! Next!'

And so, for a whole week, Imelda ate lots and lots of long foods and avoided anything that was short and dumpy. And then back she went, with her mother and father, to see Dr Anderson again.

'Next!' cried Dr Anderson. 'Next! Good heavens!' he said, when he saw Imelda. 'I've never seen such a small girl in all my days! Little girl, you should see a doctor!' And then he remembered. 'You have seen a doctor! You saw me, exactly a week ago!'

And then, just like the first time, Dr Anderson bent right down, so his nose and Imelda's were almost touching.

'Well,' said Dr Anderson, 'have you been eating your longs?'

'Yes,' said Imelda.

'And avoiding your shorts?'

'Yes, said Imelda.

'Of course you have!' said Dr Anderson. 'Just look how much taller you are already!'

'Nonsense!' said Imelda's father. 'She's exactly the same size! She hasn't grown a single jot! And you can check with your silly old wooden ruler, if you don't believe me!'

Well, Dr Anderson did check, and no, Imelda hadn't grown the tiniest jot.

'But my mother gave me spaghetti when I was small,' said Dr Anderson sadly.

'Come on!' said Imelda's father. 'We've wasted enough time here!'

They sat in a park, wondering what to do next. Imelda was terribly unhappy. Oh, she would never grow taller. She would always be small. Tiny tears began to fall from her tiny eyes.

'Excuse me,' said a voice. 'Do you sleep in a shoebox?'

Imelda looked up. It was a smiling lady.

'Well, yes,' said Imelda. 'I do.'

'I thought so,' said the smiling lady. 'My daughter was just the same. Slept in a shoebox. Wouldn't grow at all. We became quite alarmed. And then one day I found out exactly what to do.'

The smiling lady turned to Imelda's mother and father.

'Buy her a bed,' she said. 'A proper bed. Something she can wiggle her toes in. A nice, big bed with plenty of room. That's the way to grow.'

'Good heavens!' said Imelda's mother. 'We'd never thought of that. We'll do it at once!'

And they did. They bought Imelda a nice, proper bed with lots of room for toe-wiggling and growing, and at once it began to work. Imelda grew and grew, every day a little more. In almost no time at all, she was exactly the right size for a girl of her age.

And the shoebox? Do you want to know what happened to the shoebox? 'I'll keep my favourite little doll in it,' Imelda said. And that's what she did, and quite right, too. You should never throw away a good shoebox.

Published in the United States by Houghton Mifflin Company
Originally published in Australia by Oxford University Press

ISBN 0-395-48663-7

Printed in Hong Kong

10 9 8 7 6 5 4 3 2 1